THAT'S NO PUDDLE...
THAT'S ANGELA

THAT'S NO PUDDLE...
THAT'S ANGELA

Based on the television
episode *That's No Puddle...
That's Angela*, written by
Bill Braunstein

Adapted by Gerry Bailey

Illustrations by Henryk Szor

SCHOLASTIC INC.
New York   Toronto   London   Auckland   Sydney
Mexico City   New Delhi   Hong Kong   Buenos Aires

ISBN 0-439-39932-7

Produced by Scholastic Inc. in 2002 under license from Just Licensing Ltd.
© 2002 Just Entertainment Ltd/Polygram Television LLC/Mike Young Productions Inc & Digital Content Development Corporation Limited.

Published by Scholastic Inc. SCHOLASTIC and associated logos are trademarks and/or registered trademarks of Scholastic Inc.

12 11 10 9 8 7 6 5 4 3 2 1   2 3 4 5 6 7/0

Printed in the U.S.A.
First Scholastic printing, June 2002

THAT'S NO PUDDLE...
THAT'S ANGELA

THE BUTT-UGLY MARTIANS' THEME SONG

B.K.M! B.K.M! B.K.M! (ah ha!) B.K.M!
We are the Martians,
The Butt-Ugly Martians.
We are the Martians,
The Butt-Ugly Martians.

We don't really want a war.
I just want to hoverboard.
We don't want to conquer Earth.
I just want to fill my girth.

We are the Martians,
The Butt-Ugly Martians.
We are the Martians,
The Butt-Ugly Martians.

If you try to go too far,
You will see how tough we are.
If you try it anyway,
Then you're go'ner hear me say.

B.K.M! (oh yeah!) B.B.K.M! (Let's get ugly!)
B.K.M! B.B.K.M!
We are the Martians,
The Butt-Ugly Martians.
We are the Martians,
The Butt-Ugly Martians.

THE STORY SO FAR...

THE YEAR IS 2053 and the Martians have landed on Earth! The advance troops — Commander B.Bop-A-Luna, Tech Commando 2-T-Fru-T, and Corporal Do-Wah Diddy — have been sent to Earth by their ruthless leader, Emperor Bog, to take over the planet.

Back on board the *Bogstar* spaceship, Emperor Bog, along with his sidekick, the evil Dr. Damage, is waiting for his advance troops to complete the first phase of the invasion. But the three Butt-Ugly Martians love Earth so much, they have no intention of taking it over!

Instead, they hang out with their Earthling friends, Mike, Angela, and Cedric, watching TV, eating fast food, avoiding Stoat Muldoon — Earth's No. 1 Alien Hunter (or so he thinks!)—and generally enjoying themselves.

To convince Emperor Bog that the invasion is progressing well, they regularly send him fake battle reports. Meanwhile, with the help of their incredibly useful robotic canine, Dog, the Butt-Uglies are actually Earth's heroes, protecting the planet from alien attack!

B! K! M!

Sent to conquer planet Earth,
Our mission is now to protect it.
Courage to fight for freedom.
Wisdom to use these powers for
the good of mankind.
Power to defend against all invaders.

2-T'S LATEST INVENTION

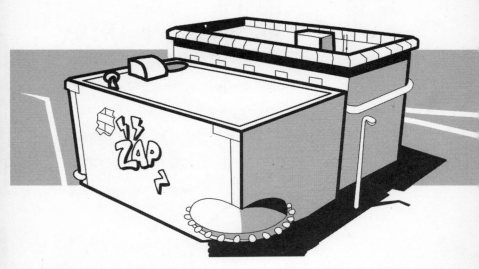

SINCE LANDING ON Earth, the three Butt-Ugly Martians have made the old amusement arcade, ZAPZ, into their very own high-tech home and work center. Here, 2-T, the Butt-Uglies' tech commando, has used his almost magical tech touch to create all sorts of amazing

1

gadgets, as well as to rebuild the old arcade games, including Doomrace 2000, the kids' favorite.

On this particular day, though, 2-T's concentration was focused solely on something new and very, very interesting. It was an odd-looking, cube-shaped device. 2-T was concentrating so hard on the new device that he looked as if he might implode! But his concentration disappeared

when he heard shouting.

"Look out!" cried Mike urgently. "Bogey at nine o'clock. Shoot!"

"Okay. Hold your horses," yelled Angela, bristling with irritation. "I know what I'm doing."

But Mike was impatient. "C'mon. Shoot!"

2-T sighed but didn't turn around. "Hey, hey, hey," he said. "Do you mind keeping it to a gentle roar? This Martian's trying to work!"

"Did he just say 'work'?" blurted B.Bop, stunned.

"Yeah, 2-T's working on some tech," said Do-Wah. "You know how he loves gadgets."

Mike wasn't about to keep quiet, despite 2-T's protest. "Shoot now!" he yelled to Angela even more urgently than before.

But Angela, playing the Doomrace 2000 game and giving it all she had, was determined not to shoot until she was ready. "Look, just. . ." she said, tripping over her words as the machine bucked and bounced like a rodeo bull, ". . . just a bit longer. Just about — now!" Angela pressed a button on the game, paused to see the result, then threw her hands up into the air, looking as if she had just won the World Hoverboard Championships. "Wooooooh!" she cried triumphantly, turning to Mike. "Your record's just become history, my friend."

"Nice game," said Mike halfheartedly.

"You just wanted me to shoot early so I wouldn't beat your record."

Mike looked amazed. "Me? No."

In the background, he could hear Do-

Wah clear his throat loudly. He could also feel the eyes of everyone in the room staring at him. "I — I — I wouldn't do a thing like that," he said sheepishly. "Honest. I swear . . ."

But luckily for Mike, he didn't have to finish. At that moment, Cedric came through the door and all eyes turned to him. He looked dejected.

"Bad news, guys," he sighed. "I couldn't get us Wingo Dingo tickets. The concert's totally sold out."

"Oh, and I wanted to see them so much," said Angela, quickly forgetting her victory on Doomrace 2000.

"Me, too," added Do-Wah. "I love Earth music."

"Do-Wah," said B.Bop seriously, "tickets or not, you know we can't go out in public. Everyone would see us."

2-T, who had been listening to the

conversation, walked over to B.Bop and the others. "Maybe . . . maybe not!" he said. "I think I've solved that problem. Ha-ha! Check this out." 2-T held out the cube-shaped device he had been working on. It was about the size of a softball. "It's my latest invention, a De-particle-izer. It will allow us to go out among humans without being noticed."

"You mean, we can go to Quantum Burgers anytime we want?" beamed Do-Wah. "Not just when it's closed?"

"Sure," said 2-T, "Quantum Burgers, the Hoverboard Park, the Mall . . . you name it!"

"What are you waiting for?" said B.Bop.

With that 2-T nodded and aimed the De-particle-izer cube at Do-Wah and B.Bop. Then he pushed a button on the side of the device. Instantly, waves of light shot out of the cube and enveloped his two comrades.

"Huh! Heyyyyy! Wooaaaaaaah!" Do-Wah and B.Bop shouted as they both melted to the floor like two candles thrown into a fire. The kids looked on in amazement as the two Martians became little more than colored puddles!

"Well, they don't look like aliens," said Mike, trying to be positive.

"Hmmm . . . must be the molecular calibrator," said 2-T slowly.

2-T made some adjustments to the

cube, then pointed it at the two puddles on the floor. More waves of light headed for the puddles and Do-Wah and B.Bop materialized back into themselves.

"Uh, nice going, Mr. Tech Commando," said B.Bop sarcastically.

"Boy, being a puddle has sure whet my appetite," said Do-Wah, grinning.

Everyone groaned at Do-Wah's joke.

"Sorry! Still, it's almost closing time at Quantum Burgers. Let's go eat!"

They all headed out except 2-T. "You guys go on without me," he said. "I need to work on the De-particle-izer."

As B.Bop, Do-Wah, and the kids headed for the burger joint, something incredible was taking place in the desert on the outskirts of the city. Under the light of a full moon, a powerful, vicious-looking alien was hard at work on his own device — a Gateway Portal. Lieutenant Penkhan, a Zvorak soldier from a distant solar system, was using his jetpack to hover in the air above the imposing structure.

The Gateway Portal was made up of a huge circular archway with a spinning energy force in the middle that glowed brightly. Stairs led up to the structure, which sat on a raised platform.

But where did the portal lead, and who was going to use it? Like a wormhole, a Gateway Portal could lead virtually anywhere in the universe, defying space and time. And this one was going to be used to transport invading troops!

Penkhan looked toward a floating audiovisual camera orb that hovered near him. He was using the shining orb to report to his High Commander.

"This is Lieutenant Penkhan," said the alien soldier. "I hear what you say, High Commander, and I'm happy to report that the Gateway and the Earth Shaker are now complete and operational."

The orb hovered just above Penkhan as the High Commander answered. "Excellent. If your Earth Shaker can destroy as much of the planet as you say, our Zvorak Invasion Force will be able to conquer Earth with minimal resistance."

"You have my word on it," replied Penkhan. Then he laughed. "There's gonna be a whole lotta shakin' goin' on!"

After eating their way through most of Quantum Burgers' food supply, B.Bop, Do-Wah, and the kids returned to ZAPZ arcade. They were curious to see if

2-T had made any
headway with
his latest
invention.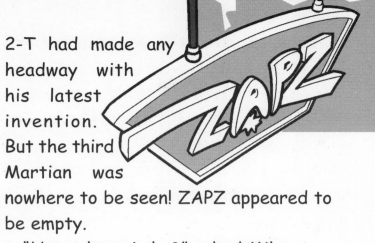
But the third
Martian was
nowhere to be seen! ZAPZ appeared to
be empty.

"Hey, where is he?" asked Mike.

First there was silence. Then 2-T's voice
could be heard coming out of thin air.
"Pssssst. Hey, I'm over here!"

Everyone looked in the direction from
which the voice had come. But all they
could see was 2-T's De-particle-izer
cube. It was bouncing through the air on
its own.

"I'm right here," came the disembodied
voice of 2-T again.

Then a wave of light shot from the
De-particle-izer and 2-T materialized in

front of everyone. He was grinning and holding his amazing invention!

"You did it!" cried B.Bop.

"Did you doubt me?" said 2-T, looking very pleased with himself.

Meanwhile, Lieutenant Penkhan had left the desert and was flying above the city, heading for a spot close to Quantum Burgers. When he reached his destination, he landed in the middle of the street, pointed his finger at a manhole cover, and fired a l a s e r beam at it. Instantly, the manhole cover began to lift until it hovered in the air. Penkhan jumped straight into the hole.

He quickly made his way down into the city's maze-like sewer system. Before long, he had reached his underground lair, which looked like Aladdin's cave, but filled with tech stuff instead of jewels. Penkhan stood in front of a large control panel — the controls to his Earth Shaker — and smiled to himself.

The device was covered in a blanket of switches, lights, levers, buttons, and dials. Penkhan worked a few of the controls and as he did so the Earth Shaker machine began to hum. He watched the dials and monitor closely. Then he grinned with satisfaction as data told him that the ground was starting to shake! "It's time to rock . . . and roll," he laughed.

Back at ZAPZ arcade, everything seemed to be shaking.

"Hey!" yelled B.Bop as they all tried to remain standing. "What the plickum?"

"It's an earthquake!" shouted Mike.

Then, suddenly, the shaking stopped.

"Everyone okay?" asked B.Bop.

They all nodded.

In his lair, Penkhan was smiling evilly at the thought of what was to come. He turned to the floating yellow audiovisual orb. "High Commander," he roared, "the test of my Earth Shaker was a success. I'll need twenty-four hours to charge it to full strength. Then we can shake, rattle, and roll our way to the conquest of this planet!"

ANGELA'S IN KIND OF A MESS

BACK AT ZAPZ amusement arcade, the kids and the Butt-Ugly Martians looked around, stunned. They had never felt an earthquake before and all agreed it was an experience they didn't want to repeat.

"Wow, heh, that was really something," said B.Bop. "Do you, uh . . . do you get earthquakes very often down here?"

"I think the last one was, like, a hundred years ago," said Cedric.

2-T was standing in front of his console, looking at a radar-type screen. "Well, according to this," he said, "the epicenter was in the desert. Hmmm. Good thing no one lives out there."

"No one except you-know-who," said Do-Wah, thinking of a certain well-known alien hunter . . . .

Somewhere in the desert, cocooned in the abandoned missile silo that was his home and headquarters, sat the man in question, Stoat Muldoon: Alien Hunter. Muldoon was in his hoverchair in front of his high-tech transmission console, holding his head in his hands. "This is terrible," he said. "It's the first night of 'Chat with Stoat' live on the Internet and we have to have an earthquake! Well, I'm hoping my fans are stalwart enough to hang in there."

Muldoon reached for a switch on the console and a screen came to life showing the www.stoatmuldoon.com logo.

"This is Stoat Muldoon: Alien Hunter and

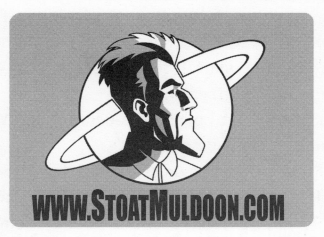

living legend!" announced Stoat. "And who do we have the pleasure of addressing?"

Muldoon listened as a filtered voice began to speak. "Call me Dark Comet," it said. "I'm just one of your legion of loyal followers. 'Keep your eyes to the skies . . . .' "

Muldoon's face lit up. "A legion? Yes, well, it warms my heart to hear that." Then he turned aside. "I hope you sponsors are listening."

Dark Comet continued, "Anyway, me and my comrades were out looking for something to report on your website, and we spotted what I think was a breach of the Earth's atmosphere. . . . And, and, it happened just before the earthquake. We think it might be related."

"Son, picking up an alien breach with the naked eye is highly unlikely," said Muldoon.

"Well, actually," said Dark Comet proudly, "I'm using a 120 digital optical-refractor with hydrogen power-boosters and 96-K oscillation enhancers."

Muldoon was impressed. "Jumpin'

Jehoshaphat! Why, that's almost as powerful as what the military has. . . ."

"Two-point-six times more powerful, to be exact. I built it myself," said Dark Comet.

"On second thought, you may indeed have found something. Rush me those coordinates and I'll investigate it, posthaste."

"Will do," said Dark Comet. "You are da man, Muldoon. Keep doin' it. Aliens don't stand a chance."

"Don't you know it, DC."

"What's DC?"

"Dark Comet."

"Oh, right. Yeah, DC, yeah."

Stoat Muldoon switched off the transmission and leaned back in his hoverchair, a look of satisfaction softening his rough-hewn features.

The day after the earthquake, Mike returned to ZAPZ arcade. He opened the door cautiously, as if he was planning something sneaky.

"Hello . . . ? Guys, you here?" he asked.

There was no answer. Mike was alone. He looked around the room and spotted

2-T's De-particle-izer. "Hah, there you
are!" he cried.

Angela, meanwhile, had gone to Quantum
Burgers, where Mike had arranged to meet
her and Cedric. She was standing outside
waiting when Cedric hoverboarded up and
landed beside her.

"Hey, Ange," he said. "Where's Mike?"

Angela looked annoyed. "That's what I'd
like to know," she replied crossly. "He tells
us to meet him here early, then he doesn't
show up. Typical guy!"

Back at his missile silo headquarters,
Stoat Muldoon sat at his console thinking
about the conversation he had had the

night before with the mysterious Dark Comet. Just then, Muldoon's Alien Tracking Device, or MATD, started to beep and flash. Muldoon picked up the device and looked at its screen. As he turned a dial on the MATD, a pulsing red dot showed the location of aliens outside.

"Looks as if Dark Comet knows his stuff," said the alien hunter as he rushed for the door. "Alien activity coming from the desert. But never you mind. Stoat Muldoon, No. 1 Alien Hunter, will protect the planet!"

Muldoon headed straight for his hovervan, jumped in, and fired it up. Flames from its wheels and the vehicle rose up through the great steel doors of the missile silo HQ. The hovervan picked up speed and lurched into the sky above the silo.

Also in the sky were the three Butt-Ugly Martians aboard their One Martian Air Bikes, or OMABs. They were flying across the desert in triangle formation. 2-T led the way but hadn't told the other Butt-Uglies what they were all doing out in the middle of nowhere.

"Hey, 2-T," said B.Bop, "what's such a big deal that you had to get us out here so early?"

"I didn't want to scare the kids," answered the tech commando, "but I picked up some strange readings last night during the so-called earthquake."

"You didn't want to scare the kids?" said Do-Wah indignantly. "How about me?"

"All right. What kind of readings?" B.Bop asked.

"A power source big enough to cause the earthquake — somewhere out here. But before I could lock onto it, it was over."

Do-Wah was *not* happy. "What exactly are we looking for?"

"Well . . . just anything unusual . . . or suspicious," replied 2-T.

"Unusual or suspicious," said Do-Wah. "Does Muldoon count?"

All three Butt-Uglies turned to look at something behind them in the sky. It was Muldoon's hovervan, approaching at speed. Sitting at the steering wheel, Muldoon was keeping an eye on the hovervan's radar screen. It showed a triangular formation of blips. Then, as he looked out of the window, he spotted the Butt-Ugly Martians on board their OMABs.

"Great balls of fire!" he exclaimed.

"Aliens dead ahead." Muldoon revved up his hovervan and headed in the Butt-Uglies' direction. "Geronimooooooo!" he cried.

"What's the plan?" asked Do-Wah as the Martians watched Muldoon heading toward them.

"We confuse him by splitting up," replied B.Bop decisively. "We'll meet back at ZAPZ."

B.Bop, 2-T, and Do-Wah banked away from Muldoon's hovervan and accelerated, leaving the alien hunter far behind them. But Stoat Muldoon was not going to give up that easily. "These invaders will learn that outrunning Stoat Muldoon is futile," he roared as he increased his speed and chased the three Martians across the skies.

Before he had a chance to catch up with them, however, the Butt-Uglies veered off in different directions, leaving Muldoon wondering which alien to follow. "So, you think you can confuse me by splitting up, eh?" he said, looking vexed. "Well, I guess you did. . . . Pretty crafty!"

As Muldoon was trying to decide which way to go, he suddenly caught sight of

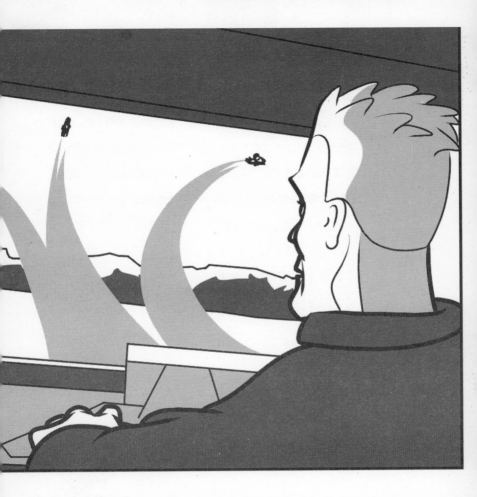

something strange in the distance. It was
Penkhan's Gateway Portal. "What the . . . ?
An alien structure!" exclaimed Muldoon in

disbelief. Then he added triumphantly, "And it's here on Earth. Today's your day, Muldoon — destiny with an alien. But hold on. It could be a mirage. Remember the last time? Oh, what the heck! Anyone could have mistaken that cub-scout troop for a swarm of invading blue Venusian midgets."

Back at Quantum Burgers, Angela and Cedric were still waiting for Mike. They were sitting at a table inside the restaurant when, finally, he walked in.

"Hey, guys," Mike said.

"Mike, where have you been?" said Angela, looking up.

Mike didn't answer. Instead he parked himself next to Angela and opposite Cedric. Then he placed 2-T's De-particle-izer on the table in front of them all. Angela and Cedric were stunned.

"Do the Martians know you have this?" gasped Angela.

Mike laughed. "Well, let's just say it's on loan."

"You took 2-T's De-particle-izer?" exclaimed Cedric, horrified. "And he doesn't know?"

Angela looked worried. "Mike, what were you thinking?"

"She's right, Mike," said Cedric. "You've got to give it back."

"Well," said Mike, "I was thinking — Wingo Dingo concert? Backstage!"

Cedric was suddenly won over. "Good point. Nothing says you have to give it back right away." He grinned.

"Oh, you guys are crazy!" cried Angela. "I mean, you don't even know if this thing works on humans. Better give it to me before someone gets hurt."

"It's all right," said Mike. "I know exactly what I'm doing."

But Angela was determined. As Mike grabbed for the De-particle-izer, she reached for it, too. In the scramble that followed, the De-particle-izer, which was pointing directly at Angela, went off, sending waves of light in her direction!

"WOOAAAAH," cried the frightened girl as the powerful light completely enveloped her.

Mike and Cedric watched in horror as Angela turned into a pink puddle on the floor of the burger joint!

"Oh, no!" cried Mike.

"Angela! Look what you did to her," gasped Cedric, looking at Mike and then at the puddle on the floor.

"Me?" said Mike. "It was an accident."

Mike looked at the De-particle-izer. "Okay, okay. Don't panic, Angela. I'll just, ah . . . reverse the process. You have nothing to worry about."

Mike picked up the De-particle-izer, aimed it at the puddle, and fired. The ray of light appeared as usual and hit the puddle. But nothing happened! The puddle remained unchanged.

"Okay," said Mike, "now you do have something to worry about!"

"Look," said Cedric, "just call 2-T. He'll get her back."

As Mike and Cedric tried to reach 2-T on Mike's communicator, they didn't notice the puddle ooze slowly across the floor and into the middle of the restaurant.

But Ronald, the Quantum Burgers' counter jerk, who was standing nearby, certainly saw it. He looked at Mike and Cedric and then at the large pink puddle on his spotlessly clean floor. He didn't like mess in his establishment.

"Someone spilled a strawberry shake on my floor," he said. "Hey, you don't get to be Employee of the Month thirteen straight months by being slow on the draw with a mop . . . do ya? Ha-ha-ha!"

As Ronald went off to get his mop, Mike was talking to 2-T on his communicator. ". . . And then she turned into a puddle," he whispered urgently.

2-T listened. He was back at ZAPZ, checking some figures on Dog's data screen, as he talked with Mike. "The De-particle-izer is set for Martian metabolism," he said calmly, "not human. But I should be able to reverse the process."

36

"Whatever you do, don't let anything happen to that puddle," interrupted B.Bop.

"We'll be right there," said 2-T, trying to sound reassuring.

Mike flipped the communicator closed, then he and Cedric turned back toward the puddle. "Don't worry," began Mike, "everything is going to be — " But he didn't get to finish his sentence. Cedric was poking him in the arm. "What?" Mike asked.

Cedric pointed at the floor of the burger joint. Mike's mouth dropped as he realized that the puddle was no longer there. It had gone!

"She's gone! Angela! OH, NO!" cried Mike as he looked around the restaurant.

He and Cedric stood and stared in shocked disbelief at where the puddle had been. They both looked as if their world had come to an end.

DROPPING IN ON PENKHAN

MIKE SIGHED AND looked up. Then he and Cedric raised their hands in horror as they caught sight of Ronald with his mop and bucket. Their brains lurched into another gear.

"Hey, hey, Ronald. Er, what did you do

with the pink puddle that was on the floor over here?" Mike asked.

Ronald looked at him as if he was crazy. "What's this, a trick question?" he began. "You don't get to be Employee of the Month by letting sleeping puddles lie. Ha-ha! I mopped it up and dumped it down the drain."

"Oh, no . . ." said Mike as he and Cedric looked deflated once again.

Meanwhile, Muldoon stood close to Penkhan's Gateway Portal in the desert, with his floating video camera in position. He was going to shoot a promotion film for his TV show. Everything was ready. This was the big time!

"All right, Muldoon," he said, "this promo ought to bring in the viewers — *numero uno*

in the viewing figures for sure. Roll tape. In three, two, one . . ." Then Muldoon turned and spoke to the floating camera. "Good day, citizens of Mother Earth. Tonight, on a very special episode of Stoat Muldoon: Alien Hunter, I'll reveal absolute proof that aliens have landed here on our planet. Don't dare miss it!"

Muldoon finished the promo and returned to his hovervan. This was going to be good.

Outside Quantum Burgers, Mike and Cedric headed for the large billboard. They knew the Butt-Uglies would be waiting there, where they couldn't be seen, and were relieved to see they had already arrived.

"You guys, we've got to find Angela," Mike said.

"What do you mean, find her?" asked 2-T. "She's a puddle. Puddles don't just get up and walk away."

"No," said Mike, "but they do get mopped up and dumped down the drain by Ronald the burger jerk!"

2-T rolled his eyes. Then he pushed

some buttons on Dog's back. "Have no fear, babe, we'll track her down, using Dog's super-scent-ometer."

Dog began to walk around, sniffing loudly.

"We just follow Dog," explained 2-T.

The Butt-Ugly Martians, Mike, and Cedric followed Dog as he walked behind the billboard. They had only traveled a short distance, when Dog stopped and pointed with his head.

"Dog's picking up Angela's scent somewhere under this manhole cover," said 2-T.

"I guess we're going underground then," said Mike.

"Do-Wah, remove the manhole cover," commanded B.Bop.

Do-Wah pressed a button on his wrist gauntlet and fired a laser beam that picked up the cover and lifted it to one side. Then Mike, Cedric, Dog, and the Martians peered down into the sewer.

Across the city, Stoat Muldoon: Alien Hunter sat inside his parked hovervan. He switched on the hovervan's monitor screen and logged onto his website. "I bet the ratings on tonight's special will blow the socks off the competition," he said excitedly. "Let's see if there are any e-mails."

As he watched the screen, the muffled

voice of Dark Comet began, "So I was right. You found something."

"You bet your sweet petunias I did," said Muldoon. "And all thanks to you. I'm going to give you credit tonight on my TV special."

"Okay," said the voice, "remember, they call me the Dark Comet. But there's no time for celebration now. I have another alien sighting. Here are the coordinates."

Muldoon looked at the coordinates and laughed as he reached for his MATD. "Son, if there was an alien down here, I'd know long before you with my sophisticated tracking devices. . . ." But Muldoon didn't get a chance to finish. "What the — ?" he yelled as his MATD indicated that there was indeed an alien close by. "Why, I'm getting a reading. And it's the same coordinates as yours. You're right once again, Dark Comet!"

"Go get 'em for me, Muldoon!"

"You bet I will, my fine, alien-hunting friend," replied Muldoon. "I'm off to protect the planet."

In his sewer lair, Lieutenant Penkhan stood in front of his Earth Shaker device and watched the arrow on the main dial.

A cruel smile contorted his face as the arrow started to move toward full power. "Nearly charged," he said, licking his lips. "It won't be long now until we can start the party."

Nearby, a light suddenly came on. It was Dog's yellow flashlight and it lit the way through the sewer for the Butt-Ugly Martians and their Earthling friends. Dog continued to sniff as he made his way forward through the dark tunnel.

"Hurry, Dog," said 2-T. "I don't know how much longer Angela's molecular system can hold on."

Just then, Dog's light revealed a large pink puddle on the sewer floor.

"I think he's found something," said Do-Wah.

"Hey, guys," called Mike, "there she is!"

The Butt-Ugly Martians gathered around the puddle to have a closer look.

"Poor Angela!" cried Cedric.

Quickly, 2-T aimed the De-Particle-izer cube straight at the puddle. A light surrounded the pink liquid and it began to glow brightly. All at once, Angela stood in front of them. She did not look happy.

"Angela, thank goodness you're all right," said a very relieved Mike.

Angela stared at Mike. "Who says I'm all right?" she said, clenching her fist and punching the air in front of Mike.

"Uh, I'm sorry. It was an accident," said Mike sheepishly.

Angela was still fuming, but luckily for Mike, 2-T interrupted her. "Guys, guys," he whispered. "I'm picking up something strange nearby — some sort of alien life."

"What kind of alien?" said Cedric.

"That's what we're going to find out," said B.Bop. Then he turned to the kids. "You guys go wait for us back at ZAPZ."

"C'mon, I'll lead," said Angela to Mike and Cedric. "I feel like I know the place." She started to walk forward, but before she got anywhere, her foot slipped on the damp floor, and she fell over a ledge and down a steep sewer tunnel. Mike and Cedric, who had followed her, slipped, too. The kids tumbled down and down the long tunnel, leaving the Martians behind them. "Wooaaaaaaaah!" they yelled as they continued to slide, out of control.

The long sewer tunnel ended in a barred, cell-like chamber. One by one, the kids dropped onto the dank ground. As they looked around, they realized that they were in some kind of prison. But beyond the bars the situation looked even worse. Staring at them, with an evil look in his eyes, was a ferocious-looking alien creature. Lieutenant Penkhan was ready to welcome his new prisoners!

"Well, look at this," he said menacingly.

"You are the very first prisoners of the invasion."

Angela looked at Mike. "The invasion?" she said nervously.

"What invasion?" asked Mike.

Penkhan laughed. "You're just in time to watch firsthand as I launch the earthquake that will begin the Zvorak conquest of your planet!"

As Penkhan talked, he failed to notice that there was movement above the cell where the kids had dropped in. The Butt-Ugly Martians and Dog had followed Mike, Angela, and Cedric and had made their way to the end of the steep sewer tunnel, just above the cell. They looked down at the kids, trying to stay out of Penkhan's line of sight. But to his horror, Do-Wah accidentally kicked a small pebble lying by his boot. The noise of the pebble falling into the cell was just enough to alert Penkhan.

Looking up and seeing the Martians, the Zvorak soldier aimed his wrist gauntlet's incineration beam at the kids.

"Hold it right there," he said to the Butt-Uglies. "I wouldn't try anything, unless you want to see your friends turned to ashes."

"Great," said Angela, staring at the alien's wrist gauntlet, "first a puddle, then ashes. Do the good times never end?"

NOW YOU SEE ME... NOW YOU DON'T!

FROM ABOVE LIEUTENANT Penkhan's prison cell, the three Butt-Ugly Martians looked down into the evil alien's lair. They were unaware that the arrow indicator on the large machine they could see was showing almost full power and that there were only a few minutes left until the destruction of Earth began!

"Look, I don't know who you are or what you want," said B.Bop, "but I do know I want you to let those kids go."

Penkhan was enjoying this. "Let me introduce myself then," he said. "I am Lieutenant Penkhan of the Zvorak."

"Well, look, 'Tin Can' or 'Oil Can' or whatever 'Can' you call yourself, if you hurt

those kids you're gonna answer to us! And trust me, you do *not* wanna go there," said 2-T defiantly.

As Penkhan toyed with the Martians, something was moving in another part of the sewer. Muldoon was heading for the same tunnel that the kids and the Martians had come down. He was carrying his Alien Tracking Device, which was beeping and glowing red. "Dark Comet was right again. There's mucho alien activity dead ahead. Careful, Muldoon," said the alien hunter.

Back in his lair, Penkhan pointed to his Earth Shaker machine and smiled. The arrow on the gauge continued to move to the red full-power point. "Once my Earth Shaker is fully charged," he said, "this pitiful planet will be nothing but rubble, and the way will be clear for our invasion!"

As Penkhan continued, Stoat Muldoon: Alien Hunter was making his way toward the sounds up ahead. He was listening carefully to the alien's ranting voice. "An invasion, hmm?" said Muldoon to himself. He went on listening as the voice of Penkhan echoed through the sewer.

"Troops from my planet will enter through our desert Gateway Portal," said Penkhan. "After that, there will be no stopping us!"

Muldoon looked dumbfounded. "That voice seems to be coming from just up ahead," he said. But as the alien hunter stepped over the very ledge the kids had slipped on earlier, he lost his footing on the steep tunnel floor. Before he knew it, he was sliding down, faster and faster. "WOOOAAAAH!" cried the alien hunter.

"Do you hear something?" asked B.Bop.

The three Butt-Uglies turned as one, their eyes growing wide as they saw Muldoon bouncing down the tunnel behind them. No one had time to move before Muldoon crashed straight down, sending them flying into one another.

"Heyyyy! Woaaaah, yaaaaah WOOOOF!" they yelled as they dropped into Penkhan's cell. Now the Butt-Uglies, Muldoon, and the kids were all prisoners!

"Do drop in," said Penkhan, delighted. "The more the merrier."

"Holy catfish!" cried Muldoon. "Aliens! They're everywhere!"

"Oh, great. My last minutes on Earth and

I've got to spend them with him," sighed 2-T.

"All right," said Do-Wah, "we're getting out of here."

Do-Wah walked up to the solid bars of the cell and put his arms around them. He heaved, pulling at the bars and using all the strength he had. But try as he might, he could not bend them.

2-T looked at the bars. "Hmm. Pretty advanced stuff."

Penkhan watched with pleasure as the Martians got nowhere. "There's no escape," he said. "Just like there's no chance for Earth." The Zvorak soldier turned his back on the prisoners and looked at the arrow on his Earth Shaker. It now registered fully charged!

"2-T, what are you waiting for?" said B.Bop urgently. "Blast 'em."

2-T nodded, pressing some buttons on

the De-Particle-izer before aiming it at Penkhan. He whistled, then shouted, "Yooooooh! Trash Can!"

As the evil alien turned, a wave of light enveloped him and a puff of smoke filled the air, obliterating him.

"That should do it," said B.Bop.

"He's nothing but a puddle right now," added 2-T.

Do-Wah grinned. "Yeah, let's not cry over spilt alien!"

The others grinned at Do-Wah's joke.

But the smiles quickly faded from their

faces. As the smoke cleared away, they could see an all-too-familiar shape. And it wasn't a puddle. It was Penkhan! Only now he looked even more powerful, and his eyes blazed red.

"Thanks for the boost," he said. "That

little device of yours is better than daily exercise. I feel stronger than ever."

Feeling utterly deflated, the Butt-Ugly Martians looked at Penkhan as if he was a Plutonian cyber ghost.

"Nice work," said B.Bop, exasperated. "What happened?"

"Well, I guess his metabolism is different," said 2-T.

B.Bop wasn't impressed. "Why is it that when your devices don't work, they end up making guys like him stronger?"

But 2-T didn't have time to answer. Penkhan walked over and interrupted them with some extremely unwelcome news. "It's time to say good-bye to this little planet." Then he went back to the control panel of his Earth Shaker and began pushing buttons. The machine started to bleep loudly. "The Earth Shaker is now activated. Time until destruction . . . five minutes and counting," Penkhan crowed.

Do-Wah looked at 2-T. "Don't you think this calls for BKM?"

2-T shook his head. "No, no. It's too risky in this tiny cell."

B.Bop agreed, then thought for a second. "I've got an idea," he said confidently as he produced a shining Electro-Magnetic Particle-izer, otherwise known as an EMP ball. "Everyone, close your eyes."

"Stoat Muldoon's eyes are never closed to the alien world," said Muldoon gravely.

"Suit yourself," said B.Bop. Then he turned to Penkhan. "Oh, Lieutenant, look over there," he said, pointing across the chamber and throwing the EMP ball at Penkhan's feet.

"I don't see anything," Penkhan said.

But as he looked around his lair, the EMP ball suddenly exploded into brilliant white

light. The alien held his eyes and stumbled around, totally blinded by the explosion.

"AHHHHH," he raged, "I can't see! I can't see!"

"That's the idea," said B.Bop with a smile.

"I can't see, either," said Muldoon, sounding mightily surprised.

Do-Wah sighed. "He told you to cover your eyes!"

2-T realized there was no time to lose. He aimed his De-particle-izer straight at Muldoon, changing him instantly into a puddle.

"What are you doing?" cried Angela.

But 2-T didn't stop to answer. He activated the device again and aimed it at the kids, turning them into puddles, too. Then, whispering to B.Bop and Do-Wah, he instructed them to push the puddles under the bars and out of Penkhan's cell.

Finally, 2-T fired the De-particle-izer at B.Bop, Do-Wah, and himself. The Butt-Uglies were now invisible.

"Over here, alien breath," said B.Bop to Penkhan.

The evil alien rubbed his eyes and

groaned. His vision was still hazy, but as B.Bop spoke, it started to clear. He looked at the cell and groaned again. It was empty! "That's impossible," said Penkhan, opening the cell door and walking into the barred chamber. "They're gone!" As his eyes searched the place, the three invisible Martians crept out of the cell and

slammed the door shut. Penkhan was now trapped inside his own prison cell!

"NO!" he shouted furiously.

2-T quickly used the De-Particle-izer to restore himself and the other Martians to their visible forms. Then he turned the device on the three kids and Stoat Muldoon, and in an instant they were back to their human forms.

Angela looked at the confusing console. "What are we going to do about the Earth Shaker?"

"Or him," added Mike as the three kids turned and realized that Penkhan had ripped the cell door off its hinges and was now free. He was standing before them, tall, menacing, and ready for battle! The kids made a run for it.

"You can't hold me," gloated Penkhan, looking gleefully at the Martians. "Your device made me too powerful."

"This may not be as easy as I thought," said Do-Wah under his breath.

And he was right. Penkhan raised his arm and activated his wrist gauntlet, shooting a dazzling photon ray straight at the Martians. The Butt-Uglies ducked and the beam shot just over their heads.

The Martians knew what they had to do. 2-T began, "Looks like it's time for" — and his comrades joined him to chant — "BKM!"

The Butt-Ugly Martians transformed into their mega-powerful BKM suits. It was

Let's Get Ugly!

a magnificent sight, and as the three of them landed in front of Penkhan, they let out their war cry, "LET'S GET UGLY!"

Penkhan could hardly believe his eyes. But he had no choice. The Butt-Ugly Martians were for real. The rattled alien activated his jetpack and flew into the air,

firing photon rays down on them. Dodging to avoid the rays, the Butt-Uglies returned the alien's fire, bombarding him with energy bolts until one winged him, and he dropped to the ground with a resounding crash.

The three Martians surrounded Penkhan as he slowly pulled himself up from the ground.

"It's all over, Penkhan," said B.Bop.

"Yeah," said 2-T, "we're putting you and your doomsday machine out of business."

Penkhan looked at 2-T and then at the Earth Shaker as the ground began to move beneath them.

"Fools," he said acidly, "I told you you'd never stop me!"

Then Penkhan touched a button on his wrist gauntlet. Below him, an escape hole opened up and he disappeared down it.

Do-Wah stared at the hole. "A secret

passageway," he said. "Let's go!"

The Martians dropped through the hole in the sewer floor and followed Penkhan.

Penkhan made his way through the sewer system. But he had not escaped the Butt-Ugly Martians. In BKM they were right behind him, firing photon rays at him from their wrist gauntlets. Penkhan managed to dodge the rays and return fire. As the battle raged on, the Martians chased Penkhan out of the sewer tunnel and into the dark night. They flew across the city and out into the desert.

Meanwhile, Angela, Mike, and Cedric had managed to find a way out of the sewer with Muldoon. As they emerged from the sewer, Muldoon spotted the disappearing Martians.

"After them!" he cried, racing toward his hovervan with the kids right behind him.

Soon they were heading into the desert as well.

"Have no fear, children," said the alien hunter. "Muldoon is on the case."

Penkhan led the Martians toward the spot where he had built the portal. When he reached it, he landed on the stairs to the portal and began to run up to the round archway of spinning light.

The Martians, who were right behind him, stopped and watched what Penkhan was doing.

"You're too late!" Penkhan cried between breaths. "In seconds our troops will be here. And there's nothing you can do to stop them!"

But Do-Wah wasn't so sure. "We'll see about that!" he yelled.

Suddenly, the Martians noticed a low rumbling sound like distant thunder, and the ground beneath them shook again. The rumbling became louder and louder as the Martians climbed up the portal stairs after Penkhan.

"The earthquake's really started now!" cried B.Bop.

"Uh, what do we do?" asked 2-T urgently.

Penkhan had finally reached the Gateway Portal, but Do-Wah acted fast. He grabbed the De-particle-izer and hurled it at the alien as hard as he could. The De-particle-izer flew through the air and bounced off Penkhan's chest.

The force of Do-Wah's throw sent Penkhan flying backward through the Gateway Portal and out of sight. But the shaking didn't stop. Instead it got even louder.

"Great shot, Do-Wah," said B.Bop.

"Now let's make sure he's not coming back," added 2-T. He quickly made some adjustments to the De-Particle-izer before aiming it again, this time at the Gateway Portal itself. The De-particle-izer threw out powerful light waves toward the portal, which began to glow and fizz with energy before it finally exploded and

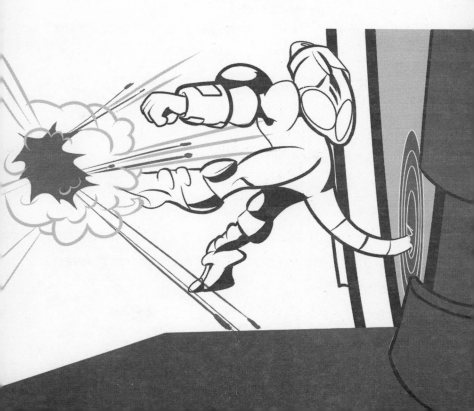

disappeared. And as it did, the shaking and rumbling stopped.

The Martians then flew over to where the kids and Muldoon were watching the

events, transfixed. Mike, Angela, and Cedric looked very relieved. So did the alien hunter.

"Good job," said Mike. "Boy, we sure owe you guys big time. You've saved Earth again."

"Again?" gasped Muldoon, sounding startled. "This is amazing! This is going to be big news — the most important discovery of the millennium. A Pulitzer prize for a very special alien hunter?"

But the Butt-Uglies were not about to let Muldoon spoil their party. They didn't want him to know they were on Earth. So they needed to make sure he would remember nothing about them.

2-T walked over to him with a Martian Memory Erase Pyramid. "I don't think you'll be winning any prizes, Mr. StoatMuldoon.com," he said, handing him the pyramid. "Hold this, will ya?"

As the Memory Erase Pyramid opened, a

colored gas enveloped Muldoon and he slumped harmlessly to the ground.

"Sure . . . aaaaaghhh," he sighed as his eyes closed, "I've been a good boy, Mommy, now can I have my ice cream, Mommy? . . ."

Later that evening, Mike, Cedric, and Angela sat at their favorite outdoor table at Quantum Burgers. Ronald had just placed six burgers in front of them.

"Ha-ha!" laughed the burger jerk. "You kids must be really hungry. I mean, I can't see how you guys can eat so many Quantum burgers."

Mike smiled at Ronald. "Sometimes, Ronald, it's what you can't see that means the most."

Then two burgers rose up from the table and floated in midair. Ronald looked at the

burgers as if he had been slapped in the face with a wet pizza. "What the —?" he mouthed.

Even as he watched, he heard a loud chomping noise and the two Quantum burgers disappeared.

"I think I'll have three more," said the voice of Do-Wah.

"I think I need to lie down," said Ronald as he turned on his heel and ran away.

Angela, Mike, and Cedric threw back their heads and laughed as the Butt-Uglies materialized. The sound of their laughter could be heard across the street — along with the belching guffaws of three other individuals crammed full of Quantum burgers. . . .

HAVE YOU JOINED THE BUTT-UGLY MARTIANS ON ALL THEIR ADVENTURES? DON'T MISS ANY OF THE ACTION. BUTT-UGLY MARTIANS #1

The Big Bang Theory

Muldoon has captured Dog! Now the Butt-Uglies and the kids are on a highly hazardous rescue mission. Things get even worse when the kids encounter a Nitchup, a seemingly harmless alien who will explode if exposed to Earth's atmosphere—too bad no one thought to tell Cedric that before he freed the little guy. Can the Butt-Uglies save the day?

BUTT-UGLY MARTIANS #2

Meet Gorgon

Emperor Bog has sent the Butt-Uglies
a brand-new weapon: Dr. Damage's
Molecular De-atomizer. Unfortunately, a
weapons-thieving, shape-shifting alien named
Gorgon has stolen it—and captured Mike and
the Butt-Uglies! Now it's up to Angela and
Cedric to try to rescue their friends. Can the
Butt-Uglies break free and finish off the evil
alien? Or have they finally run out of luck?

Help the Martians save Earth!
LET'S GET UGLY!